Billy
Of No Use At All

By
Neal Evan Parker

All rights reserved. No portion of this book may be reproduced without the author's permission. Reviewers may use short passages for the purpose of written or broadcast commentary.

Publisher's note: No animals were harmed during the writing and production of this book.

ISBN 9781440476181

PRINTED IN THE U.S.A.

©2008 Neal Evan Parker

Published by Annabel Books
P.O. Box 252 Rockland, Maine 04841
www.schooneryacht.com
207-594-1751

Billy
Of No Use At All

**By
Neal Evan Parker**

For Annabel.

    With true friends you will always find your way...

Love, Papa

Chapter 1

"Oh, dear. Doctor, are you sure?"

"As sure as sure can be, Mrs. Peasoup. Though your daughter's condition is rare I've seen it before. And the tests never lie."

Mrs. Peasoup turned to the sweet faced gangly girl across the room. "Billy, would you please excuse the doctor and I? Perhaps you can find an interesting magazine in the waiting room, okay?"

The eight-year-old girl slid from the waxed-paper covered exam table with a sigh. She had been to too many doctors, excluded from too many conversations during her young life. "Yes, mom."

When Billy had closed the door behind her, her mother again turned her attention to the pediatrician.

"Dr. Kindly, are you certain there's no way she can see us through the wall?" asked Mrs. Peasoup.

"No, she cannot," replied Doctor Kindly.

"Can't hear us from the waiting room?"

"No, Mrs. Peasoup, she can't. And Billy can't hover outside the window and spy on us either. We have complete privacy," the doctor assured.

"How did this happen?" Billy's mother asked with a sob. "How could she be born with no super powers? I mean none whatsoever." Mrs. Peasoup regained her composure and continued, "It certainly doesn't come from my side of the family. Now her father's third cousin…"

"Mrs. Peasoup, it doesn't matter what the reason. You'll make yourself crazy trying to figure it out. The important thing is that your daughter is— how do I put this, though very bright, she's defective. Children like Billy are of no use at all and contribute nothing to society. Anyway, the law requires me to report all defective children to D.O.N.O.S.P. if they haven't developed super powers by the time they reach her age." D.O.N.O.S.P. was the Department Of NO Super Powers.

Mrs. Peasoup dabbed her eyes with a hanky and peered through the wall. She could see Billy reading quietly at the end of the hallway. "She looks so, so normal. Are you sure it isn't an allergy—"

"We've been through this." Dr. Kindly interrupted.

Billy's mother focused her gaze from her daughter to the D.O.N.O.S.P. poster on the wall. At the center of the floral design was a message that was loud and clear.

D is for, *Don't* worry.

O is for, *One* child more or less won't matter.

N is for, *No* way is anything going to change.

O is for, *Once* your child is eight there is no hope.

S is for, *Sayonara* baby.

P is for, *Prepare* to give up your child.

It was hard for Mrs. Peasoup to read those words without quietly humming the jingle that was part of the public service commercial.

"Mrs. Peasoup. Mrs. Peasoup?" said Doctor Kindly, trying to regain the mother's attention.

"Ah yes, doctor. I guess I was just lost in thought watching the children in the playground across the street."

Doctor Kindly peered through the outside wall of his exam room. The kids out there were flying loop-de-loops around the monkey bars, laughing with glee. Kindly could tell it would take a bit more effort to quell this mother's fears.

"Don't worry, Mrs. Peasoup. You are young enough to make another child."

"Thank you, doctor, I suppose Mr. Peasoup and I will get right on that... Sadly, however, he *was* attached to this one, even though she never was quite right."

Doc Kindly produced a warm grin. "Don't either of you worry about Billy. She'll be just fine. It's not like the old days when children like yours were barbarically kill... well, I'm sure you know the stories. No. Since the advent of space travel the world government has come up with a much kinder method of disposal."

Mrs. Peasoup's pink lips widened. "Yes, when I first heard about it I thought it was science fiction. Now they send children all the time to that place where no one has super powers. What was that called again?"

"Earth," the doctor winked encouragingly. "Certainly that's where she'll have the greatest chance of leading a normal life."

"Have you ever been there, doctor?"

"Oh, no. No one has actually been there. We've just been pointing the *Rockets of H.O.P.E.* in that direction." The doctor swiveled around in his stool to reach for a color brochure which he picked up and handed to the mother. "Here, Mrs. Peasoup, this should explain everything."

The mother looked at the tri-fold pamphlet. Pictured on the front was a bulbous rocket ship gliding effortlessly through space. Through the large single porthole shone the face of a happily sleeping youth that was neither boy nor girl. Announced, in bold yellow letters against the starry black was *Rockets of H.O.P.E.* Underneath it plainly spelled out, *H*elping *O*ne *P*erson *E*vacuate.

"You have been so kind, doctor. So what happens now?"

"I'll have my secretary call D.O.N.O.S.P. and they'll send an officer to pick Billy up. In the meanwhile I suggest you slip out the back door. We have it just for this sort of nastiness. Goodbyes can be very traumatic for all parties."

Chapter 2

"Excuse me, miss. I'm Broderick from the Department Of No—" began the heavyset man in the pea green uniform.

"Yes, yes," said Doctor Kindly's receptionist from behind the sliding glass window. "You are here for Billy Peasoup." The secretary slid the window aside and pointed into the waiting room, "She's right there reading a maga— that's funny. Where could she have gone to?"

Broderick looked around at the coughing, wheezing, feverish children attended by their out-of-sorts parents before he proclaimed. "She must have run away, ma'am, that's what these kids do. It's okay, though. She can't fly, she won't get far."

With that the officer from D.O.N.O.S.P.

flipped a switch on his hat producing a flashing green light on its crown. Then with the tinkling of glass Broderick took off out the window. Even the kid whose eyes were sealed shut with conjunctivitis watched with the others, all using their super vision to trace the green-clad officer's path across the sky.

"Where is the policeman going, mommy?" wheezed an asthmatic boy. It was the question that was on all the children's minds.

"It's none of our business what the police do." retorted the mother, battling her own curiosity. "Now go fill that bottle the way the nurse told you to." But as the boy moved to open the bathroom door, out popped Billy, who, knowing Officer Broderick was gone, made for the exit, hoping not to draw attention to herself.

Outside, the young Billy Peasoup took in a breath of fresh afternoon air. She suspected there would not be many more days for her as sweet smelling as this one. It was only a matter of time before she was caught and sent away forever.

Overhead people swished back and forth, off to shop or to visit friends, to work or whatever most people did on a Thursday afternoon. The crumbling remains of the sidewalk were seldom used anymore except by defective kids and their worried parents who dragged them from one doctor to another. Billy sat down unhappily on a curb where once in a while various people landed near her and bustled into nearby buildings.

The young girl thought of her life, and of her father. How could he allow her be sent away without at least saying goodbye?

She knew there was a severe penalty for any parent who did not follow the rules of D.O.N.O.S.P., but not even a farewell?

"If only I could see him one more time," Billy sighed to herself, "then for all I care they could stick me on any rocket to any place they liked." But that wasn't how Billy really felt. She tried to be strong but she knew inside that she didn't want to leave home, her father or her mother. As little Billy fought her tears she began to feel that funny sensation in her head again. It had first appeared only weeks before. This time it was swirling pictures, first of her father and then of a green uniform... Wait! What was that swishing sound? Without being sure why, Billy stood, prepared to run away and would have but at that exact moment a thick shadow suddenly fell over her.

"Well, young miss. I was half hoping you would be giving me a harder chase. But I've got you now," declared Broderick, switching off the light on his hat and speaking to his radio. "We need a wheeled transport unit to bring in a defective on the corner of Lexicon Avenue and—"

Billy only half-heard the officer, for thoughts of her father were growing stronger. Then suddenly there was a familiar noise, like the rush of wind in a tunnel, and the next thing Billy felt was herself being carried quickly skyward.

"Daddy!" the girl called out, her cheeks flapping in the wind.

"Yes, dear it's me," comforted Mr. Peasoup.

"But where are we going?"

"To show you the truth. Now keep your eyes and mouth closed. I'm about to speed up to make sure we escape the police."

Billy knew her father was an athlete from back when he was a student at the Academy of Science. No way was that chubby old Broderick going to catch them in the air or on the ground. Happy in her father's arms Billy did as instructed and held tight knowing he would keep her safe.

A short while later Billy's father landed in a part of the world where a chilly night had already begun. The two large moons were almost full, casting a shadowless luminescence on the unfamiliar landscape. Billy, a bit wobbly from her ride, looked around trying to make sense of the strange place.

"We don't have much time, Billy, so I'll start to explain before your mother gets here."

"Mom's coming? But I—"

Billy suddenly became silent, for at that moment her eyes were drawn to a disturbingly familiar structure. Its three fins supported a bulbous container which swept up and around a single porthole like an elongated teardrop ending with a sharp menacing stinger. "That's one of those *Rockets of H.O.P.E.!*" Billy gasped. "You and mom *are* sending me away!" The tears flowed as she turned, hiding her eyes from her father.

"No, dear, no," Mr. Peasoup tried to console his daughter with a hug but she pushed him away. Clearly she would rather cry on her own than in the arms of a liar.

"Okay, Billy, listen to me. There is no such thing as a *Rocket of H.O.P.E.* The whole thing is made up. A fake. A fraud.

This is the only rocket and it's part of *this* place. Something they used to call an amusement park."

Billy was listening but was not yet willing to lower her hands from her face. That would depend on what her father said next."

"Please, pay attention. As I mentioned, your mom will be here soon. Really. But I need to know you are listening because your life, our lives depend on what happens next.

Okay, Billy thought. *I guess this is pretty important.* She turned to her father, drying her cheeks. "Okay, dad. Tell me. What is this place?"

"It's called an amusement park. When I was a little boy, before the big Change happened, the world was full of places like this. Parents used to bring their children to— well, for example, do you see that crazy-shaped railroad that does all those twists and turns against the sky? That's called a roller-coaster. Kids used to get in those small cars there at the bottom, shoot along the track and scream their heads off... And that, that thing with the beautiful wooden horses. It's a carousel. I can still remember the joy of going round and round and up and down."

Billy was spellbound. "What does that one do, dad?" she asked, pointing at an immense circle with once brightly painted swings. Except for the rocket the big wheel was taller than anything else in the park.

Before her father could answer Billy felt a tingle announcing her mother's arrival. Landing, Mrs. Peasoup spoke softly. "It's called a Ferris wheel, sweetheart. It was my favorite ride, especially one year when the motor broke and my own mother and I got stuck at the top for hours."

"Mom!" yelled the girl, throwing her arms around the woman who she had truly believed had abandoned her but who now planted a dozen kisses on her face and head.

"I'm so sorry I left that way, Billy. I had to act in that despicable manner or arouse the doctor's suspicions. He can't know your father and I are part of this."

"Part of what?" puzzled the girl, who followed her mother's eyes to Mr. Peasoup.

"You haven't told Billy yet? We have so little time," Mrs. Peasoup said with alarm.

"We haven't been here very long because I had to zip by way of the South Pole to make sure that pesky D.O.N.O.S.P.

officer couldn't track us." explained Mr. Peasoup.

"Okay," interrupted Billy. I can see I am going to have to be the adult here. Will somebody please tell me what is going on!"

"You *are* going to have to be a grownup and I am sorry that it has had to come so fast," began Mr. Peasoup. "So here goes. As I started to tell you, this is the sort of place that your mom and I used to come to when we were children. But after the Change, all that, well, changed. When people began flying and doing for themselves what all these thrilling machines used to do for them, this sort of playground was no longer needed."

Mrs. Peasoup interrupted, "Tell her why things changed."

"It might be best if you do that," father muttered sheepishly.

25

"Oh, no!" Mrs. Peasoup was quit resolute. "You're the scientist. You were part of it. You explain this to your daughter."

Billy's father took a deep breath, snatched up a couple of toppled plastic chairs and beckoned his daughter to sit with him. Mrs. Peasoup grabbed a third chair and, joining the two, watched Billy's face as her father took her hands. With another deep breath he began.

"It really began as a joke when I was in college. You see, the world was on the verge of ruin because there was almost no fuel left to run factories, heat homes, make cars go. More and more people were starving, food couldn't be harvested and the stuff that could, well, there was no way to move it to the stores. With me so far, Billy?" Mr. Peasoup searched his daughter's eyes, which encouraged him to continue.

"Okay, so my classmates and I were in the laboratory one day talking about the fuel problem and wondering what every scientist in the world at that time was wondering. That was, whether or not we could find some way to invent an energy source to keep our cars and planes and all the machines going. Well, I forget who, but someone jokingly suggested that we were trying to solve the problem the wrong way and that what we really needed to do was reinvent people. Super humans who wouldn't need cars and jets or who could run factories and make electricity by running in wheels like hamsters. Well, of the six of us in the lab, not one of us laughed. This bad joke really did seem to be the answer. A year later we had our first breakthrough. We injected a monkey with— well, I won't explain the scientific formula, but that monkey started to do amazing things. He didn't live long, though. All that extra power kind of burned up his body. So we refined our mixture and the next monkey lived... a bit longer. Well, word of our experiments got out and soon it seemed every scientist on the planet was competing to come up with a formula that would work on *just* people. You understand, the thought of super bugs and super lions and such was too frightening.

"To make a long story short, it was a team of biologists from the southern lands who came up with the final solution." Mr. Peasoup let Billy's hands slip from his own as he was suddenly disgusted by his own participation in what had led to the greatest scientific boondoggle of all times.

"Without further testing or warning, the world government loaded this chemical onto anything that could fly and quite literally sprayed the planet. The effects were almost immediate. Suddenly people were freed up from needing cars and trains to get around. The air was cleaner and—"

Mrs. Peasoup interrupted, "But a problem was discovered."

Chapter 3

"The problem was that not all couples were passing these super powers along to their children and injecting the kids directly didn't seem to work either." Billy's mother looked sympathetically at the seated girl. Mr. Peasoup continued his wife's train of thought.

"The government started calling these children different, then defective and after a time began convincing parents that, in order to keep the world from sliding back to the disaster it was, their defective children needed to be sent away. That's when the leaders in government created the Department Of NO Super Powers. It was to take these children and—" Mr. Peasoup couldn't bring himself to say it, so he paused and continued the story from a different direction.

"D.O.N.O.S.P. began a campaign which convinced everyone, well, most everyone that these defective children were not only of *no use*, but a threat to humanity.

"Most parents gave up their defective children and didn't ask questions. But there was a growing number of parents who did ask. That is when the Rockets of H.O.P.E. program was founded, to create the belief that the children were being sent to happy lives on a planet a billion miles away."

Billy's mother cut in. "Honey, the truth is there are no such rockets. The Department Of NO Super Powers used a picture of an old amusement park ride and placed it in a fancy brochure. I mean, look at it," Mrs. Peasoup said, pointing at the spaceship, "it's such a friendly looking rocket."

Billy worked hard to digest all this startling information. "So why did you bring me here, to show me a rocket that doesn't work? And what are they really doing with the other kids? What are they going to do with me?"

Billy's father stood, again taking his daughter's hand in his. Leading the family towards the spacecraft Mr. Peasoup explained, "We don't know what's happening to the other kids. There have been some dreadful rumors. But whatever it is, Billy, such will not be your fate. This rocket here I am about to show you is kind of special."

"Dear, your father has been working

very hard to prepare it for you."

"You are sending me away? But this thing is a fake. You just told me so."

"No," said Mr. Peasoup, as they arrived at the futuristic contraption. "It used to be a fake. Now it's sort of a hybrid."

"A hy-what?"

Mother explained, "A hybrid. Kind of a blend of this and that, which your father has been scrounging from home and the junkyard. It has plenty of food and air on board if you remain asleep for your journey. And since there is no rocket fuel anywhere in the world, your daddy has come up with an ingeniously simple way to launch it."

Billy didn't know much about rockets but knew enough to be concerned. "How *will* you launch it?"

"Well," began Mrs. Peasoup, "we, your father and I, that is, are going to, well, lift it past the clouds and just before we run out of breathable air we'll give it an extra shove into space. Isn't that right, father?"

Mr. Peasoup gave a nod.

"And mother, father, just how long will I have to sleep for? I mean when will I get to the other planet?"

The parent's eyes met, with looks that begged the other to answer. Mr. Peasoup finally said, "Depending on how much speed your mother and I work up before we let go, it shouldn't take more than about five hundred years."

Billy began to cry, throwing her tiny arms around her father's waist. "I don't want to go. Why can't I stay here with you and mom?"

Mrs. Peasoup got to her knees and hugged her child. "Dear, please, there's no time for tears. The police are searching for you and your father as we speak. You have to leave before they find this place. And once we take off we have to be fast because the moment we leave the ground the world radar system will find us and then—"

"That's quite enough," interrupted Mr. Peasoup. "No need to scare Billy with unnecessary details." Then fighting back his own emotions he told his daughter, "Now listen, don't think of it as a rocket. Think of it as a lifeboat. It's sturdy and up to the task of seeing you to safety. And everything is automatic, the food, the thingy that puts you to sleep. Everything. Understand?"

Billy nodded, dried her eyes, hoping

to appear brave and even smiled. "Okay, dad, mom. But if I get to Earth and change my mind I can come back to you, right?"

The proud parents smiled lovingly at their brave little girl but Billy suddenly felt a tingle and sensed there was something more she wasn't being told. As her parents reached to unlock the spaceship's hatch the eight-year-old insisted, "One of you better tell me what you're not telling me or I'm not climbing aboard."

It was Mr. Peasoup who took up the task.

"You are right, dear. You need to know all. The government wants everyone to believe you and all the kids like you are defective. But they *are* hiding something. The truth is, they are worried because the children with no apparent super abilities, far from being defective, are superior, vastly superior. Billy, it's already happened to kids older than yourself. In a few years, when you have matured a bit more, your brainpower will be greater than any of the super-strength people on our planet. You might even be able to read minds. Do you know what that means? It means, to a government that wants to stay in power, super-smart kids are very dangerous. They grow into super-smart adults. If the leaders didn't dispose of your kind you could end up being the new rulers of the world.

"Now sweetie, you have five hundred years to think about what your father just told you. Time to get aboard." encouraged Mrs. Peasoup.

"I'm ready," Billy declared with a

faraway look in her eye. Moments later she was buckled up and peering out the rocket's porthole. With a thumbs-up to her mom and dad, Billy Peasoup signaled that she was ready to begin her long journey.

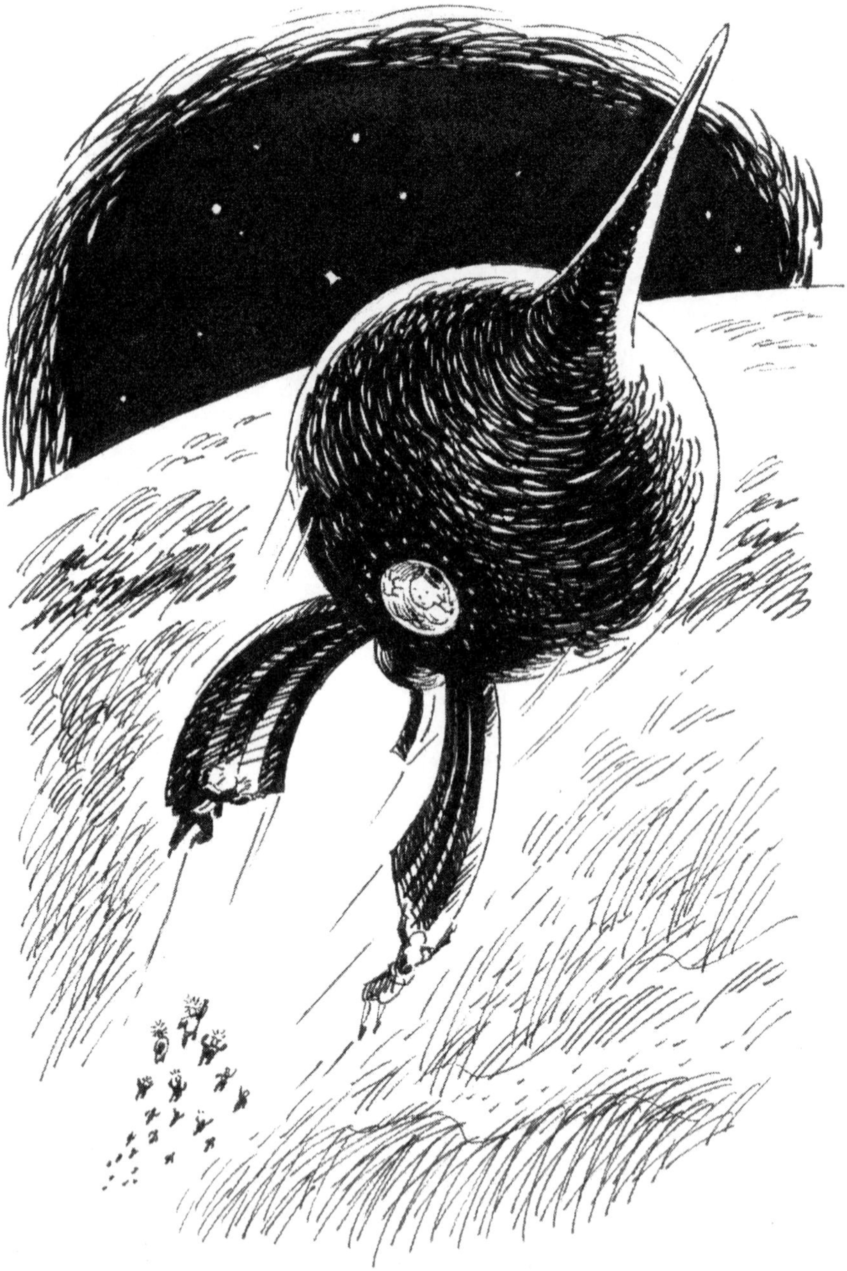

Chapter 4

The rocket had barely begun its climb skyward when hundreds of beeping radar screens lit up at World Headquarters. Commotion ensued as the alarmed skywatchers at O.O.P.S. bounded in excited confusion against the computers, walls and ceilings and finally each other as they rushed to leap out the windows. O.O.P.S. was the governmental agency established to watch the sky for Offensive Outsider Penetrating Spacecraft. There had never been any real threat but now, at last, a large unidentified metal object showed up on radar in a sparsely populated part of the world. That could only mean one thing, only no one knew what that one thing was.

Feeling useful at last, the agents of O.O.P.S. zipped off to investigate.

Meanwhile, high above the abandoned amusement park, the only true Rocket of H.O.P.E. was gaining speed. Peering out, Billy watched her parents, each of whom was clutching one of the spaceship's fins, lifting with all their strength. Reaching the clouds for the first time, Billy found herself reciting a little ditty she remembered from kindergarten:

There once was a girl lost in space,

Whose fear was so plain on her face.

What had started as fun,

To fly towards the sun,

Ended up as a crispy disgrace.

All young children were cautioned about the dangers of flying too high. A warning that Billy had never had to heed until now. And why should she worry? Her parents always looked out for her.

Suddenly the girl sensed the tingle of danger at the same time she saw her parents glance worriedly to the distance. Even if Billy had not seen the looks of concern on their faces she trusted her senses enough to know something bad was fast approaching.

As the girl feared, a flying army of government agents with their blinking green lights was rapidly approaching. Billy felt the rocket lurch faster, then faster still as her mother and father gave it every bit of oomph they had. The worried girl pounded on the glass yelling, "Stop, Mom! Stop, Dad! Get away or they'll catch you!"

Her parents forced comforting smiles. Truly desperate, they pushed even harder while gulping a last dose of life giving oxygen just before reaching the blackness of space. They held on until the color left their cheeks and the life drained from their once super powerful arms.

The agents of O.O.P.S. paused above

the highest cloud watching the rocket speed away. They knew better than to leave the safety of the planet's thin blanket of air, so they watched and waited to see what would happen next.

As the rocket hurtled towards the distant stars Billy tearfully saw her frozen father, then mother slip away and begin their fall back towards the planet like lifeless mannequins. Seconds later the scorching heat of her parent's descent caused their bodies to streak like shooting stars against the blue-grey planet below. Gaining control of her emotions Billy sniffled and bravely muttered:

> *There once was a girl lost in space,*
> *Whose fear was so plain on her face.*
> *But her parents said 'Love,*
> *We will give you a shove,'*
> *But they wound up a crispy disgrace.*

Billy was reciting and refining her new poem when a sweet smell entered the cabin of her craft. And then she was asleep.

Even with the last powerful shove her parents had given the rocket it was still another week before Billy flew past Zowee, the eighteenth and final planet in her solar system. It is just as well that the eight-year-old, in her deep slumber, missed the dark clump of rotating ice. She might have been further saddened by the realization Zowee would be the most interesting thing she would see for many years to come. A month after Zowee slipped from sight Billy's own home sun was a mere pinprick in the vast darkness.

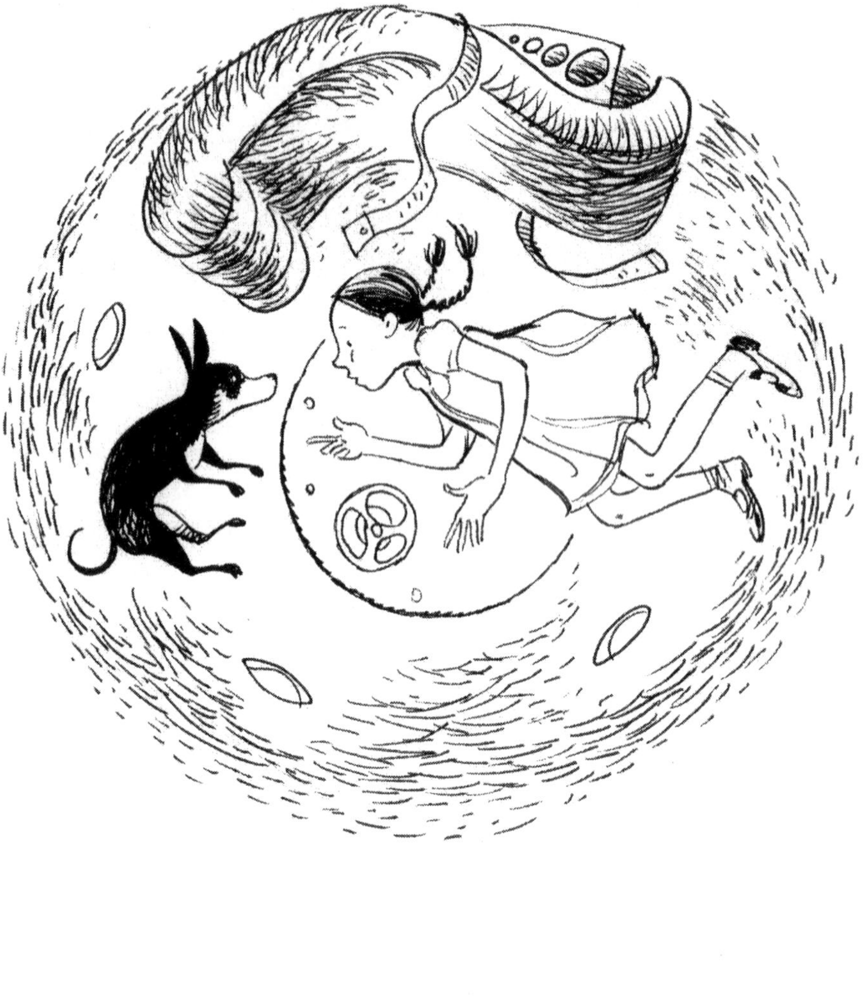

Chapter 5

The metallic clang was so loud that Billy, who was long lost in her artificial slumber, quickly opened her eyes. Her sudden awakening was made easier by the spaceship's automatic system which, in the event of an emergency or arrival on Earth, shut down drowsy mode and turned on a mist the smell of which Billy didn't like at all.

The girl, now fully alert, flexed her stiffened limbs. What's going on? How long have I been asleep?" she thought. Billy did not expect an answer but one came anyway.

"Ha! Asleep at the wheel! I should have expected that much. And who's going to fix the damage to my ship?"

Not sure if she was imagining things, Billy peered out her porthole. It took some neck twisting but at last she saw it. Towards the top of Billy's rocket, another craft lay smushed like a deflated squeeze toy.

"Who are you? What are you doing here?" Billy shouted, rapping on the glass.

"Ouch, my poor ears! Don't shout. I'll come to you," came the reply.

"I'm not going anywhere," Billy thought.

"Certainly not until you get my spaceship fixed," Billy imagined hearing.

While waiting for the appearance of her unknown guest the girl again wondered how long she had been sleeping. "It must have been at least..." Glancing at her watch Billy stopped cold. She tapped her wrist repeatedly, hoping it would correct the faulty timepiece. "Six years? It can't be. I mean it seems just yesterday I was with my mother and—"

Billy heard her rocket's hatch open and close. She felt a draft as the cold of space tried to invade her ship. Seconds later a furry weightless visitor drifted in.

"Six years in space, you say? That's nothing. I must have racked up at least that much just going back and forth to Canis Major. That's where I was coming from when you made me smack into you." The creature's long mouth, which sat beneath two pathetic eyes, never moved once as it spoke, nor did his stubby tail wag to signal any desire to be friendly.

Billy gasped, "You're a dog. Some kind of terrier. But what…?"

"First of all, I asked you not to shout. We are close enough together that thoughts will do just fine. Second. Thanks for calling me a terrier. There's parts of this universe where they call my kind 'rat dogs' and worse. Anyway, let's get the introductions over with, okay? I got a lot of other dogs counting on me. Lives are at stake. Understand? Capiche? So. My name's Gilbert and if you care about exactitude, I am not just a terrier. I'm a Min Pin."

Gilbert studied the dumfounded expression on Billy's face. "I'm a Min Pin. A Miniature Pinscher? Didn't you ever hear of...? Aw, geese. They're letting anybody into space now. So who are you, kid? And don't shout."

Billy was at a loss to respond. How could that question be answered? Just eight years old when her parents gave their lives to save hers, the orphaned girl was now suddenly fourteen but had aged hardly a day because of her deep deep sleep. Her confusion was apparent as she also wondered, "Who's this dog who can talk to me through my mind. Is that his doing, my doing or what?"

"Both," Gilbert interrupted with a

cautious wag of his stub. He was starting to feel sorry for this confused girl. "It doesn't matter what part of the galaxy a dog comes from," the pooch explained. "We all communicate with our minds. Sure, on some uncivilized planets canines haven't evolved past barking to make themselves understood. But you, kid, Billy if I read you right, you have a highly advanced frontal lobe. Lucky for us because I've tried the barking thing. Had to when the war began but I have to tell you, I don't like it one bit."

"I was headed for earth—" Billy stopped to recall the awful moments of her departure. Gilbert, giving a small push off from the wall where he floated, skidded weightlessly to nuzzle his face against the girl's stomach.

"So sorry about your mom and pop, kid."

"Thanks," Billy whispered, giving the

dog's ear a gentle scratch.

The Min Pin caught himself starting to thump and pulled away. "Okay, missy. We're getting a little too touchy-feely here. Let's get back to the rocket problem. Don't think for a minute your sad tale, some sympathy from me and a bit of ear scratching is going make me forget about the need for you to repair my ship!"

"But I don't know anything about fixing ships or rockets or any of that. Anyhow, I'm not so sure this was my fault. I mean, look out the window. Seems to me that your rocket has bumped into mine. Not the other way around."

Gilbert moaned and licked his chops. It was an effective way for him to hide his true thoughts while he engineered a response to the shrewd girl.

"Well, this isn't about one space traveler

blaming another, is it?" asked Gilbert.

"No. Not if you put it that way," apologized Billy.

"Right! I mean accidents do happen, don't they? The point is, my young rocketeering friend, that my vessel has been damaged in an accident and yours has not. Seems to me that—" the Min Pin didn't have to finish. Billy already understood the crafty dog's self-serving logic.

"You think that it would be only fair for me to help you," smiled the girl, beginning to think it would be nice to have company even if it were only for a while.

"Young miss, you are a mind reader!" cheered Gilbert.

"Yes," Billy replied. "I'm starting to think you're right."

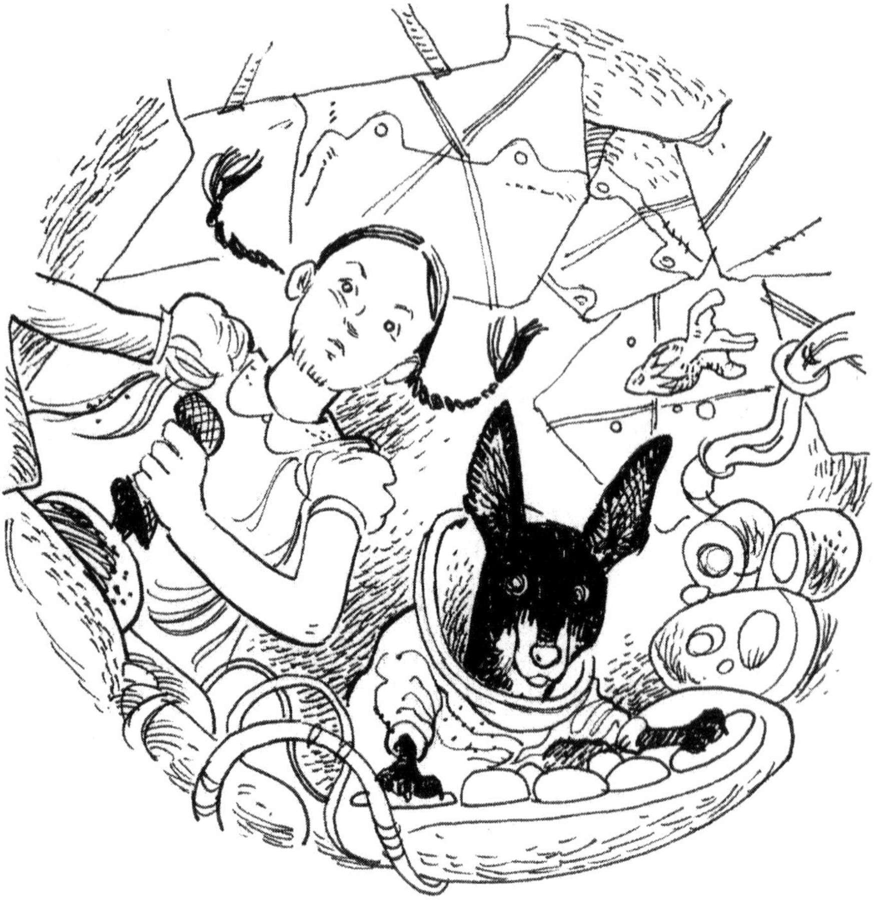

Chapter 6

Gilbert, hovering in the vacuum of space, attached the last booster rocket to Billy's ship.

"That should work. Give it a try!" the dog tele-communicated with enthusiasm. The tough little pooch was bundled neck to boots (four of them) in a wrinkled metal suit. Around his head was an oblong glass globe that fogged with every moist breath. From the top of his headgear came a set of robotic jaws which did the work his helmeted mouth could not.

Billy looked out the porthole to make sure Gilbert was at a safe distance before pushing the new buttons inside her capsule. A split second later four tiny blasts issued from the sides of the girl's spacecraft, propelling it forward.

"Nice work, Gilbert," Billy congratulated. "All we have to do now is cut your ruined ship loose, get you back inside here and be on our way."

"Not so fast," the Min Pin responded. "There's a couple of important items of a personal nature I need to retrieve, then I'll be ready to go. And yes, Billy, I have *more* stuff, so stop your complaining. It just makes you like all the other two-foots in the universe."

Billy was not used to this mind-reading thing. There must be some trick to keeping her thoughts private that the dog knew but she had yet to learn.

Waiting patiently for Gilbert to gather his effects, the girl looked around her very cramped rocket. It had not been all that spacious to begin with but now every corner, it seemed, was packed with cases and boxes of canned and dried dog food and assortments of boxed treats. Then there was a slobbery round yellow thing that drifted to and fro looking like maybe it had once been a tennis ball. Billy gave a breath in its direction for fear it might start coming towards her.

Returning inside Billy's rocket Gilbert announced, "Can't live without these!"

"What is that disgusting thing?!" But Billy already knew as she stared at the filthy pillow which Gilbert floated into the cabin. "That bed of yours better not have fleas—"

"Funny thing, that. They can put a dog in space but they can't get rid of fleas. How's that for technology!"

Billy felt like scratching just at the

thought, but she was too consumed already with a second item. One that the pooch kept clenched in his teeth. "And just what is that?"

Gilbert chomped the pasty-colored object in his mouth several times proudly demonstrating its marvelous squeak. "This, young lady, is a dream," began Gilbert letting the object go so Billy might better inspect it. "This was my first chew toy. It's shaped like a little spaceship, see? Okay, it's seen better days but when I was a pup, well, this *toy* set my imagination on a path putting me where I am today."

Billy tried not to roll her eyes and fought the impulse to even think of a sarcastic remark to make to the dog. Still, he caught enough of her brainwaves to have his feelings hurt. Quickly grabbing up his squeaky thing the Min Pin shot back, "Well I can see you never had a dream about doing something or you'd understand." Billy was too embarrassed to apologize. The dog was right. To cover her thoughts the girl cleared her throat and discovered that when she opened her mouth the dog could not read her mind. That made sense to Billy because experience back home told her that mouths often interfered with thoughts.

"Okay, girly. Time to get down to business." Gilbert picked at his left ear where his spacesuit had been chafing. A tuft of hair flew from his nails. "Ah! That's better. Now look. You talked me into going along with your plan. Let's review it one more time."

"Wait. That scratch. That wasn't a tick or a flea, for goodness sake, was it?"

Billy demanded to know before going any further.

"That's for me to know and you to find out," grunted the dog, using a few squeaks from his chew toy for emphasis.

"That's why dogs use those things!" Billy suddenly realized.

"That's right, kid. As long as our mouths are wrapped 'round one of these, no one knows what we're really thinking. Now, can we go over the plan, please?" insisted the dog.

"Alright," transmitted Billy. "First let's recap. After inspecting your spaceship you determined it was too damaged to repair. So I suggested we attach your propulsion system to my craft, which didn't have any means of locomotion at all. Now we have one super-duper rocket that can get us anywhere—"

Billy paused a moment. She didn't realize how much she had come to dislike the word *super*.

Gilbert, listening in, consoled, "That crazy world is all behind you kid."

"You're right," Billy agreed. "Now where was I? Ah the plan... So, we will fly our super-duper rocket to your home planet, which is currently ravaged by a war between the dogs and the cats."

"Ahem," whined Gilbert, "you say that as if dogs and cats are equals. Not so."

Billy gave a funny little sigh, "I suppose you're right. You are not the same. As you explained it to me, the cats are beating the dogs, big time. Anyway, you yourself have no right to be so high and mighty, it's not like you are helping your fellow canines escape out of some sense of duty or the goodness of your heart. To hear you tell it, you're making a small fortune."

"Well, I'm taking a big chance, girly. Do you have any idea what the Cat Patrol would do to me if I'm caught? It's torture, I tell you. Most of the secret police are Siamese and they *never* shut up. I hear rumors that even when they question you they don't stop mewing long enough to hear you answer. So you see, I am taking a tremendous risk and deserve compensation. Anyhow, there are plenty of my kind who are perfectly happy to cough up a hundred pig's ears to be flown to a world that's safe."

Billy shrewdly replied, "Sounds to me like it's the pigs that should be trying to escape more than anyone."

"Really," decried the Min Pin. "Well, I see we are getting way off topic here. Let's just agree to disagree and move on."

"Okay," granted Billy before resuming her recap of the plan. "So, we fly back to your world and pick up as many hounds as we can fit—"

"Terriers is what you meant to say, I'm sure. Hounds are two solar systems over."

"You're right, of course." Billy spoke so the dog wouldn't hear her think what she really wanted to say. "Moving on. We sneak into orbit and drop down to your secret landing spot. You load as many of your furry friends aboard here as possible, then we re-launch while praying that we can get past the Cat Patrol again. If all goes well we zip over to the other world and drop off your passengers."

"That's right," Gilbert joined in. "Then I fly you to Earth, depositing you there the way your parents wanted. In exchange you let me have this nifty ship to keep."

"I still don't understand one thing," Billy questioned. "You say we can reach Earth in a couple of days but my father told me it would take, like, five hundred years."

"Sure, if you are tossed into space like a fetch stick it's going to take forever. I mean that's not enough speed to reach anywhere in a reasonable amount of time," Gilbert explained. "But if you have the latest technology, well, that's another story. And that's exactly what my booster rockets got. Of course I don't expect a two-foot to understand how it works, being so scientific and all."

Billy's reproachful look at the pooch said, "Try me."

"Alright. I'll do my best to make this simple. We use a system called, Frisbee—" the dog wagged.

"F.R.I.S.B.E.E.? What does that stand for?" If you consider the world the girl had come from it was reasonable for Billy to ask.

Gilbert was puzzled. "It stands for nothing, kid. Frisbee is exactly what it is. Look at it this way. What happens when you toss one of those things? I'm sure you know. Any *dog* knows. You got to run faster than the Frisbee, right and at the last second wheel around and catch it midair, right? Well that's kind of how our rockets are designed."

Gilbert could see his new partner trying to visualize his explanation.

"Alright let me put it another way, If the motion of an object is represented by the letter A and the distance it needs to travel is represented by the letter B then by combining the two and multiplying by a factor of six you get your speed. See?"

Billy, pondering the dog's math a moment, questioned, "What if you multiply the inverse by a factor of seven. Would you increase your speed?"

"Yeah, I heard that's what the cats tried," mused Gilbert, "but their rockets went so fast they shook apart. When that started happening it could have given us the edge we needed to win the war, but our *Alpha* males were so busy infighting we missed the chance."

There was silence in the cabin as Gilbert thought of the opportunity lost and Billy pondered a planet of full of cats and dogs fighting like cats and dogs.

"Well then," Billy commented in their telepathic connection, "we better get the show on the road."

With Gilbert pawing the newly installed control panel and Billy at the jury-rigged rudder, the countdown began. The time it took for the companions to recite backwards from ten to one was a mere fraction of the time it took for Billy's renovated Rocket of H.O.P.E to reach a speed, the terrier claimed, was in excess of twenty trillion miles per second.

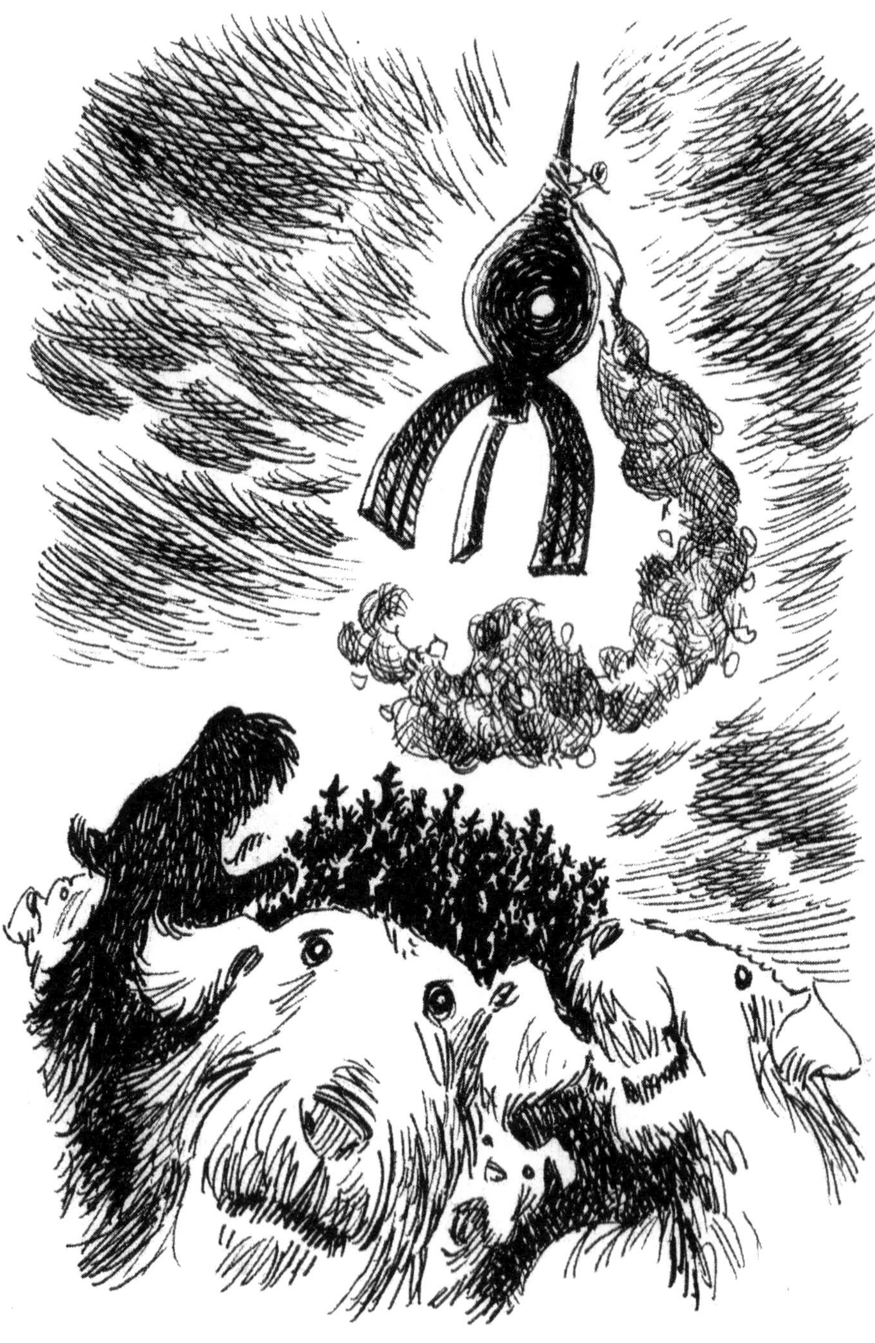

Chapter 7

"Isn't it beautiful!?" Gilbert exclaimed, looking down at the planet he called home.

Billy, edging the dog away to peer out the porthole, studied the black and white orb below. Grey clouds hung in wistful swirls, making it hard to tell where land ended and water began. "There's no colors?" Billy questioned.

"No what? What are colors?" the pooch shot back, as if insulted that his co-pilot didn't appreciate the raw beauty she was now privileged to behold.

"Never mind," Billy said, using her spoken voice.

"Now listen." The Min Pin was suddenly very serious. "We have to be extremely careful not to get anywhere near the dark side of the planet. That's the part ruled by the cats. We keep to the light, it hurts their eyes. Got it? They usually cross over between dusk and dawn for their attacks. They're nocturnal hunters, you know."

"I don't get it," Billy said, adjusting the rudder. "How can one side of your world be dark and the other side have a night and day?"

Gilbert held one front paw stationary and made sweeping motions with the other as if drawing on air. "Imagine this here is how my world spins around the sun. See? One side is always dark. Now *our* sun, unlike most stars, instead of giving a steady light is a kind known as a *Pulsar*, that is to say, it flashes slowly off and on. When it's *on* it's day and when it's *off* it's night. This is how it's been since before civilization. But three years ago the news reported that the nights were getting longer and longer."

"Your sun is dying?" Billy didn't really

have to ask. It seemed a reasonable assumption.

"That's right. With less daylight the cats have become emboldened to take over. Every night brings attacks which take more of the world away from us dogs," Gilbert brooded before returning his attention to the business of the spaceship. "Okay, now. I'm going to slow us down. You steer for a low thick cloud and stay in it. I'll take over from there."

Billy steered as the pooch instructed but continued to mull over their conversation. "Something I don't get. If everybody knows the sun is dying then why isn't everyone trying to get away?"

Gilbert shoved two levers with his nose and pawed the helm while cursing, "Cats are lazy good-for-nothing bums. Pounce, eat, sleep. Pounce, eat, sleep. That's all they do. Hey, did you hear the one about the calico and the can opener? There's this calico, see…"

Billy didn't listen. Though not knowing why, she didn't care for this sort of prejudice. Instead she focused on how well the Min Pin maneuvered the spaceship into low orbit above a windswept mountain. Beneath the craft the stony peak seethed with moving dots. Suddenly Billy's mind was scorched with cries for help. She then realized with dismay that each of those moving specks was a dog desperately calling out to be rescued. As the ship dropped even closer the girl could distinctly make out the different terriers. There were the wirehairs, the shorthairs, the curly-coated and more. Waiting almost patiently were the distinguished Kelly Blues. Finally Billy noticed three sobbing soft-coated Wheaton puppies who had been separated from their mother.

"Good gracious! There's thousands of dogs. We can't save all those!" Billy gasped. "I mean, we might be able to squeeze six or seven in here but that's pushing it. Oh, it's so sad!"

"Ha! You underestimate this Min Pin," wagged Gilbert. "Here, take the controls and keep the ship in this spot." With that the pooch climbed down to the bottom of the rocket and opened the hatch. Then, bearing a large bundle of ropes, Gilbert bravely climbed outside and after a dewclaw-breaking climb shackled the cable ends to the spacecraft's long pointed nose. Within minutes a tightly woven web draped around the ship and dangled to the ground. Billy, looking out her porthole, realized that the meshwork was covered with hundreds of large foil doggie bags. "Good dog, Gilbert." thought Billy, "way to go!", but the busy pooch did not answer.

The moment the webbing was dropped to the mountain the Min Pin climbed to within reach of the hordes of frantic canines and began to sell tickets. Soon his pockets were bulging with hundred-pig's-ear bills, which in fact were worthless because the dog government never backed them up with real pig's ears.

Terrier after terrier paid their fare, climbed up and slipped into a silvery sack. When zipped, each bag held just enough air for the voyage to the new world. But as spaces filled rapidly, mayhem and desperation took over. Pushing and shoving turned to out-and-out pawfights until Gilbert was no longer able to handle the frantic crowd. Billy shouted in her loudest thought, "Gilbert, grab those puppies, they don't stand a chance!"

"But they don't have any money!" the Min Pin objected.

"Get them, now! I'll find a way to pay you! Go, fetch!" Billy ordered. There were so many dogs thinking at once it was hard to tell if Billy had gotten through to Gilbert. But then she saw him leap boldly from the web, grab all three pups in his mouth and scamper back to the ropes. In short order the whining babies were squirming at Billy's feet. Gilbert threw the girl a sour glance. "They're not my responsibility. You're the one cleaning up after them." Before the girl could answer, the Min Pin climbed down, slammed the hatch shut and howled telepathically, "Hit the red button! We're getting out of here!"

Billy did as told. Quickly the rocket began its shaky ascent. Those dogs without benefit of the silver suits held the web as tightly as they could. But, as the rocket continued to accelerate, the poochs' strength gave out. One by one the terriers who had not paid plunged to the ground below, failed in their hope to reach the new world. A chance they were willing to take even if unprotected against the ravages of space. Anything was better than waiting for the cats to come.

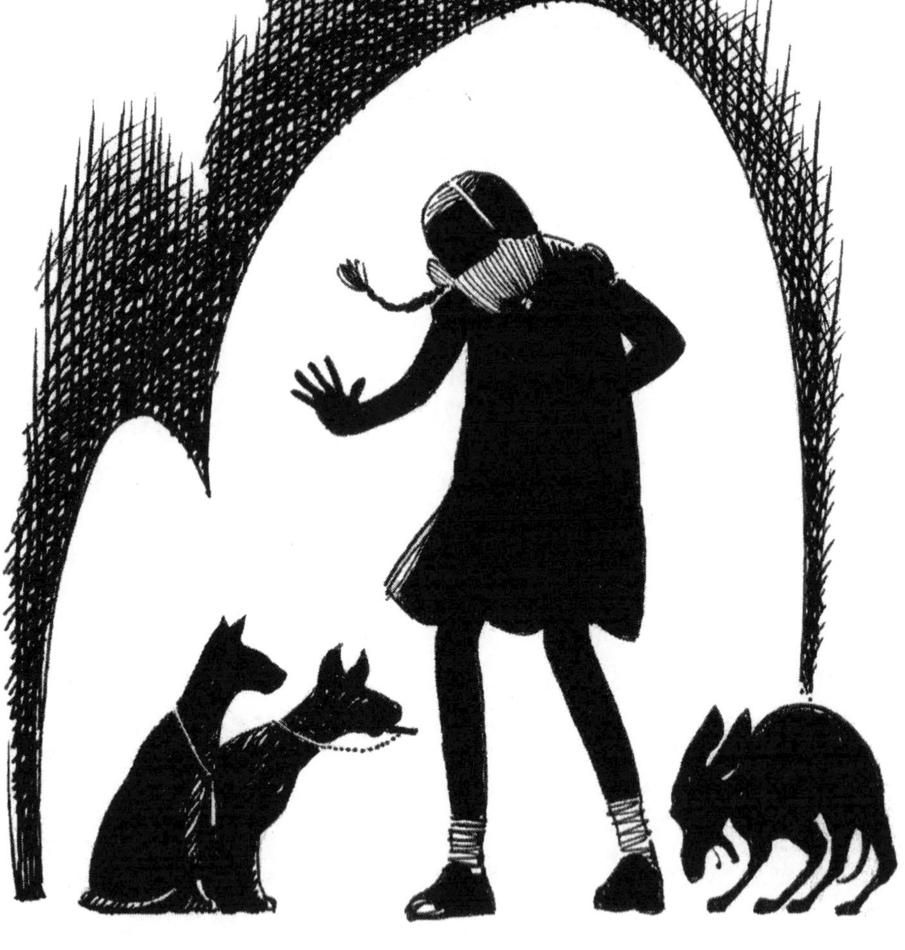

Chapter 8

The whole ugly business made Billy feel sick. She let Gilbert pilot the ship while she sat quietly, mouth open to hide her despair. From outside she could hear frightened whimpers coming from the canine cargo that covered the rocket and even trailed behind where the nettings hung past the vessel's fins. In another few minutes the ship would be clear of the atmosphere and exposed to the bleakness of space. It was all so horrible.

Billy looked down towards her feet. The three puppies, with eyes half open, crawled playfully over each other in a pile of fur. "There," Billy thought with a sad smile creeping to her lips, "is the promise of the new world."

"I heard that," growled Gilbert. "Nice

sentiment, but we ain't out of the fenced-in yard yet. Look there, just below us. That thing coming up fast. That's the Cat Patrol. And let me tell you, where there's one ship there's usually more."

"Can't we go into that super-duper drive and get the heck out of here?" Billy asked desperately. The girl had so enjoyed watching the pups she had foolishly ignored the warning tingle in her head.

"Not yet. We need more altitude. With the weight of all the refugees outside it's going to be tough to keep ahead of the catships. I hope to Dog we make it."

"I have an idea!" Billy cried.

"Don't shout! Okay, what's your idea, 'cause we're going to have to do it fast."

"Well, since we can't lighten the ship on the outside let's lighten it on the inside. We might be able to toss out enough weight—"

"Whoa, there, two-foot. You aren't thinking of throwing any of my stuff overboard! That's prime canned dog food. Do you have any idea what I'm going to be able to sell that for when we land these other terriers on the new planet? Anyway, what am *I* going to eat?" Gilbert had his priorities.

Billy, not waiting for the Min Pin's approval, was already opening the hatch to dump the food. Still, she felt the need to convince her partner. "Gilbert, if we get caught what do you think the cats are going to feed you?"

The girl's comment hit home, for in an instant the pooch placed the speeding craft on autopilot and jumped below to help Billy dump the thousands of cans of Apollo Prime Cuts Dog Food which came in an assortment of mouth-watering flavors.

Billy's idea soon proved brilliant in a way she had not dreamed of. As the food was tossed out the hatch the cardboard boxes disintegrated, spraying the spaceship's wake with the hard metal cans. "Look, Gilbert!" Billy thought excitedly. "The catships are trying to dodge the food!" No sooner did the Min Pin look up from his task than a glimmering jumbo-size container of Hearty Horsemeat smashed through the nose of the lead catship, sending the wicked craft into a tailspin.

A resounding cheer came from the canine refugees strapped to the Rocket of H.O.P.E. They had been desperately watching the five, now four catships that were in hot pursuit. But for Billy and Gilbert there was no time to congratulate themselves. With the chance of escape renewed they tossed dog food with abandon. Beneath them now, the thinning atmosphere was littered with bursting boxes and scattered cans.

The catships dodged and weaved but still gave chase. But then a second pursuer was struck and was forced from the hunt. And another cheer went up from the refugees.

"Those other three, they're stopping! They're giving up!" gasped Billy.

"Yep, that's cats for you," smirked Gilbert. "They're sprinters. You know. They can go real fast for short distances. No endurance for the long haul like us dogs—"

If only Billy and Gilbert could have enjoyed their small victory. But just then their spaceship lurched unexpectedly to a stop, sending those inside and out headlong in all directions. Gilbert, hitting his nose against the tiller, wailed, "Did I mention that cats are very good at pouncing out of nowhere?"

*****

It was uncomfortably dark inside the H.M.S. *Cheshire,* giant flagship of the entire cat fleet. The place stank terribly, which while irritating Billy's nose did not have the same effect on Gilbert. Like most dogs in the universe he was enticed by the sweet scent of cat litter. But despite that small pleasantry there was no comfort, for he, his partner in crime and all the other refugees were leashed in the bowels of the orbiting enemy flagship. The mass of frightened fur whimpered in fear of the short future they imagined in store for them.

"Well, Billy. At least we got some of them before they got us." The Min Pin had no remorse for his actions. Just the opposite.

"I'm not ready to give up," Billy flashed back. "I don't know what these cats have in store for us but I'm—"

Suddenly the mass of terriers let out a pained howl.

"Ow, stop it! Please make it stop!" barked Gilbert and the others, leaping at their chains and trying to cover their ears.

"What is it?" Billy cried out in grave concern.

"Don't you hear it? *Ow!* It's getting louder!

It saddened the frightened girl to see her companion in such agony, barking like a common stray. But then Billy saw the cause of the unbearable pain. Standing in the darkness by her feet were two pairs of winking orbs. Barely silhouettes, the cats looked up at the girl suspiciously. Each feline dangled from its neck a sparkling silver whistle. The kind only dogs can hear.

Each of the felines spoke in turn *at* Billy, but the girl could not make heads or tails of what they were saying.

"I don't understand. I have no idea what you're telling me."

"Don't bother," remarked Gilbert snidely, regaining his composure. "There's no communicating with cats."

One of the felines raised his whistle, aiming the full force of its high-pitched blast at the disrespectful Min Pin. Instantly he pinched his tail between his legs and began anew to bark for mercy.

Gilbert's embarrassment at having his dignity stripped away tore at Billy's heart.

"Stop! STOP!!!" the girl shouted with

the full strength of her lungs. "I don't know what you want from me but just leave him alone and I'll do it!"

The cat stopped blowing its whistle and Billy was immediately unleashed and lead away.

Chapter 9

Led through the dark ship Billy soon found herself deposited on the poshly appointed command center for the entire cat fleet. Half a dozen felines lazed about twitching levers and knobs with their tails while their narrowed eyes sleepily watched a wall-size telescreen displaying the world below. Things were distressingly quiet until one cat, with a diamond collar, eyed Billy, crossed to the prisoner and began to twine around her ankles.

"Akkkk, akkkk, akkkk," the cat chattered repeatedly.

Billy tried to communicate in both words and telepathy but neither seemed to work. Soon another cat rose and began to twine and chatter, then a third. Soon they were all upon the perplexed girl. Some continued to twist, turn and rub while others stretched to her knees, yawning with sharp open claws.

Billy kept still, nervously wondering what to do as the cats' movements became more aggressive. Sharp curved nails started to pull at her clothes, then her skin, causing red gashes to appear on her legs. More and more frenzied the felines became, until one leapt to Billy's shoulder, claws digging into her neck.

"Ouch!" Billy complained, trying to knock down the aggressor. But her swat at the first cat didn't stop a second and then a third from leaping up and drawing blood. Billy, now under attack by crazed felines, shouted futilely. "Get off, I am not a bag of catnip—" but every time she wrangled one to the floor it clawed its way up again. "—I don't want to hurt you!"

Finally Billy had enough. She grabbed the cat with the jeweled collar and was about to hurl it across the room when a booming hiss brought the attackers to a complete halt. Looking up, Billy saw the telescreen had changed from displaying the planet below to a surreal image of a stone-eyed Russian Blue feline. Smoke orbited the animal's disembodied head while lightening cracked all around the god-like figure.

Billy was quite startled by the mysterious image but had barely time to study it before the Russian Blue issued another lordly command. "SCAT!"

The half-dozen cats which had been torturing her scattered in all directions, coming together briefly to escape through the one and only exit from the bridge.

With the ship's command center cleared of all but the girl, the feline on the telescreen let out a hearty laugh then pleasantly chuckled, "Well, *they* won't be back for a while, that is... until curiosity gets the best of them."

"Who are you?" Billy demanded of the image on the screen. "I can't even read your mind!"

A hinged panel suddenly opened in the bottom of the telescreen wall. "That's because I'm keeping you from doing so," came a small voice. "Permit me to introduce my real self. I am Algernon. And, as you have by now observed, I am a mouse and not really a vicious Russian Blue, leader of the cats. I only play him on TV."

Billy, looking down at the snowy-white rodent, held her mouth agape.

"I see that you've learned," Algernon began, observing the girl's open jaw, "how to hide your thoughts too."

But Billy, getting over her shock, had no desire to hide what she was thinking. She wanted to give the little creature a piece of her mind.

"I don't know what you think you are trying to accomplish or why Mr. Algernon, but if you are the one responsible for attacking my ship and torturing all those poor terriers then shame on you!"

"First of all it's not Mr. or Miss or Mrs. Algernon. I am just Algernon. I'm not male or female or perhaps I'm both. "

If the mouse's comment was meant to distract Billy from the real issue at hand, it worked. "Well then, what are you?"

"I am a specially engineered laboratory mouse. If it's easier, you can call me a whoosamawhatsis or whatever suits you. I was created by beings like yourself to see if chemically treated foods were safe. When those tests were over, leaving me sicker than you could possibly imagine, I was..."

Algernon began to rattle off his extensive resume, which ranged from surgical procedures to being forced to wear makeup to insure it was safe for people. In experiment after experiment the mouse proved himself to be a survivor. Then one day he was sold to a group of scientists who, as Algernon explained, "were working on a way to give people super powers but it didn't turn out the way they had planned. Instead I became a genius."

"Wait a second!" cried Billy. "You're not from—"

"Yes!" the mouse shouted excitedly, completing the girl's thought. "The planet with two moons just six years west of here!" The two shared a moment's thrill at such a chance meeting but then, remembering the occasion of their meeting, a more serious mood ensued.

"So, young lady, how is it you have come to be on Woof World? Get it? Kind of catchy, don't you think? Okay, it needs some work."

"You might say I too am the victim of a failed experiment."

Billy recounted what her father told her about their planet before her birth and went on to tell about her life, her parents and her escape. Finally Billy described her encounter and subsequent friendship with Gilbert and how the two came to be prisoners on the *H.M.S. Cheshire*.

"Hey, you'll appreciate this since we come from the same place. H.M.S. stands for *H*is *M*ouse's *S*paceship. Good, huh?"

Billy gave a weak laugh. She was too concerned about Gilbert and all the other captive dogs to find much if anything funny. She did find the odd mouse companionable enough but since he still commanded the cats that made him very dangerous. Billy did not attempt to hide her feelings which the rodent heard loud and clear.

"Listen, you want all those dogs freed? Consider it done, doggone it!" smiled Algernon.

"Do you really mean it?" Billy choked down her excitement. "Swear you mean it!"

"Hold that thought. I hear my officers returning. Just stand here and don't move a muscle." Algernon dashed back behind the trap door. Two seconds later he popped his head out again, this time wearing a tiny mask which looked convincingly like the stone eyed Russian Blue. The mouse's voice was muffled by the disguise as he instructed Billy, "Oh, yeah. Don't overact but try to look frightened, okay?" With that Algernon dashed out of sight and reappeared on the screen just as his feline captain and her subalterns stepped cautiously onto the bridge. When they had all entered, the telescreen boomed, "Akkkk, akkkk, akkkk."

The cats paused and chattered amongst themselves. It seemed they didn't like what they were commanded to do but as soon as the Russian Blue shouted "*Scat!*", (throwing some lightening bolts for good measure) the hesitant captain and her juniors left the bridge.

Algernon popped out through the trap door, lowering his mask. "It's getting harder and harder to control those beasts. We may only have a few minutes."

"Tell me quick then," urged Billy. "Will you really release me and the other prisoners?"

"I'll go one better. I'm coming with you.

I've been trapped on this ship for more years than I care to think about. I didn't want to start this war but it was them or me!"

"By them you mean the cats, right?" Billy asked.

"The cats, the dogs. It's all the same. Everyone in the galaxy is aware of the feline species relationship to mice, but do you know what terriers are? Rodent hunters. Rat dogs, to the less linguistically blessed. That's what they've got the long nose for. Didn't know that bit of canine trivia, did you!" The mouse looked Billy in the eye. The girl shook her head, admitting she was not up on her dog facts.

"Anyway, my being here all came about because of the last experiment I was subjected to. You see, back home things were so desperate that anyone with a little science background was trying to find answers to questions that weren't even being asked. Like I was explaining, when I was injected with the formula that was supposed to give me super powers I didn't get any. Instead I got the super smarts, like you. But I didn't let anyone know I was a brainiac because I figured that was the smart thing to do. Those practitioners of pseudoscience might have tried to open up my head, you know, surgically. I had seen it done to my cousins. To make a long story short, I played dumb and since I was of no use anymore I was sold to a laboratory that launched me into space hoping to figure out how much air I breathe. What a bunch of idiots those endowment-grabbing researchers were. Wouldn't surprise me if next they tried to figure out how much wood a woodchuck could chuck if a woodchuck could chuck wood."

Billy interrupted, "So, that explains how you ended up in space. How did you get way out here?"

"Now, that's the kicker." The rodent mused. "Seems those scientists made a little error in the navigation. Instead of sending me up forty-six miles, the supposed geniuses sent me forty-six million. Well, I had no windows in my rocket so I can't be sure of how far I had traveled but after a long nap I felt a thump. I woke up and here I was, shipwrecked in the middle of what I thought, at first, was a world of just dogs."

"Wait," Billy interrupted suspiciously. "Why didn't your ship burn up as it entered the planet's atmosphere?"

"Ha! Little miss. You are not so clever as you think you are." The mouse grinned. "It took my superior mind little time to figure that one out. You have probably noticed this entire planet is black and white?"

"Yeeessss...?" Billy dragged out.

"Well, what is fire?"

Billy responded, "The result of friction between atoms?"

Algernon rolled his eyes like a frustrated teacher. "No, no, no! Think outside the exercise wheel. Your answer is too complicated."

"Well, what then?" Billy honestly wondered.

"Alright, I'll tell you," the mouse began. "Fire is red!"

"Red?" puzzled Billy.

"Red," stated the mouse again. "And that's why my spaceship didn't burn up. If you don't have red you can't have fire and therefore—"

Billy was quite dumfounded by the mouse genius's explanation. Rather than let him prattle on she interrupted by clearing her throat, "Ahem. As you said, the cats could come back here at any time. Can you hurry to what happened next?"

Algernon was happy to comply.

"Well, as I was saying, I exited my ship and found there were rat dogs everywhere. And not the type we find back home but highly advanced ones capable of space travel and all that. Well, I spent the next year dodging, escaping, surviving and wandering. Those beasts can be very aggressive. Seems they never sleep. A couple of times I tried to form an alliance with the local mice but they were not only cliquish, but they proved well beneath my intelligence.

"Anyway, my extensive travels brought me to the edge of the dark side of this world where I discovered the cat rule began. Then and there I knew what I had to do. The only way I was going to survive this nutty place was if the dogs and cats were kept busy with a nice war. So I broke into the headquarters of the biggest newspapers on both sides and started publishing stories reporting that there was less and less daylight and that soon the entire planet would be dark all the time. Well, it didn't take long for the news that cheered the cats to cause dismay and panic amongst the dogs. Those brutes, unlike the independent cat types, have a pack mentality, so they required no guidance from me. But the felines, they needed a leader who would organize an all out effort to take over the planet.

"Anyhow, without going into too much detail, I made my way aboard this ship and built myself a hidden command center which, to be honest, is more like a miniature television studio. It's where I run the war from. I created the Russian Blue dictator character but didn't need to create a dog leader because as I said, unlike cats, dogs are a pretty self-motivated bunch." Algernon looked quite pleased with himself.

"You horrible, horrible rodent. How could you do this? Who knows how many are dead because of you!" Billy felt the rage growing inside.

"Whoa there. Back up!" waved Algernon frantically. "No one's died that I know of. Certainly no more than usual. Gee whiz. Give me a little credit. I'm not that kind of mouse."

Billy seethed, "What do you mean by that?!"

"My war is very carefully orchestrated. Kind of like a catch and release program.

Okay, it works like this. The dogs, in their panic try to escape on those rockets like the one used by your profiteering friend. Only thing is, I am tapped into their navigation controls. Gilbert and his sort are not flying to some far-off world with their passengers. No. They are just landing in a desolate spot of my choosing on this one. Meanwhile the cats capture as many of the escaping refugees as possible and at my direction bring them close to where they started from, only neither side is the wiser. It wouldn't surprise me if some of the same dogs have been captured two, three, maybe more times than that!"

The mouse was so serious in his explanation that Billy was forced to believe him or her.

Billy leaned close to the rodent and narrowed her eyes. "So, what you're saying is that you have created some kind of evaporation cycle only instead of water it's raining cats and dogs? And you have done all this why?"

"To survive," answered Algernon defensively. "As long as they are all kept busy with this war neither canine nor feline will have time to chase the likes of me…"

Billy felt that Algernon was not quite finished. "I think you were about to say *except*. Except *what* exactly?"

"Except, as you may have noticed, some of the cats may be starting to catch on to my game, though they haven't figured out the whole truth. That's why I'm leaving with you."

"But what's going to happen if you abandon the cats and leave them leaderless? What will happen to the dogs?"

"I've long prepared for this day though

I didn't know exactly when it would come. As we speak a news story I prepared is hitting the papers and televisions telling both sides that there was a misprint and the world is not coming to an end. That should stop panic amongst the terriers. I expect they will, with a renewed vigor start to defend their territory again rather than try to run away. As for the cats, well, without a strong leader like me they'll happily slink off to life as it was before. Alright. No more questions. Time for us to scram!"

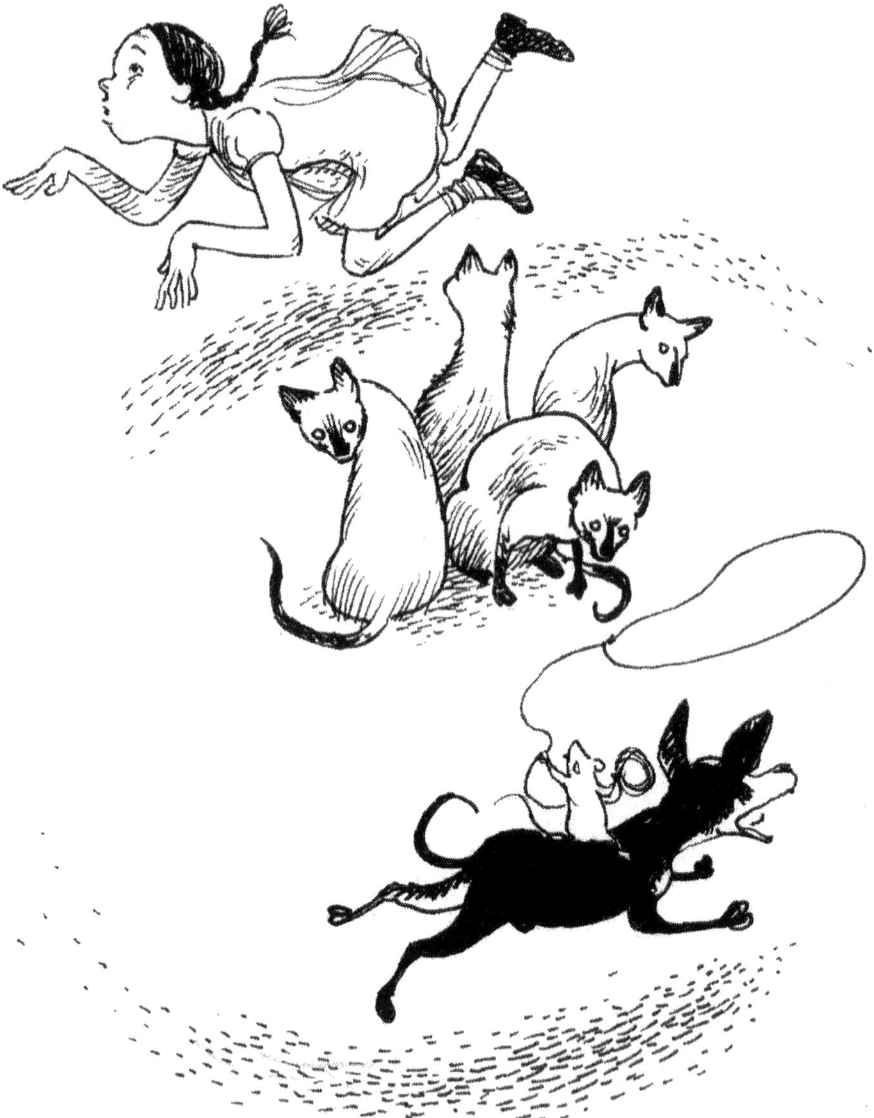

Chapter 10

With Billy keeping as low as possible and Algernon leading the way, the two sneaked from the bridge down to the prison of the flagship. During this transit the rodent proved his remarkable intelligence by following the maze of compartments in a way that avoided discovery by the cat crew.

Gilbert, upon seeing Billy safe, was so excited that he almost wet the deck. And he might have if not for suddenly catching sight of the mouse. That triggered an instinctive reaction, one that involved growling and gnashing of teeth.

Algernon, who himself was not above a good fight, quickly calculated the tensile strength of the chain leash, the force already upon it and the dog's weight. Satisfied the canine could not break free the mouse blew a loud raspberry and cried, "Rat dog!" Algernon's loud insult drew the attention of all the other terriers causing a wail of protest and a number of unspeakable insults.

"Look," Billy said, scolding her fighting companions, "we three have to get off this ship and we are going to need each other to do it."

"She's right," sighed the former leader of the cats. "The H.M.S. *Cheshire* will land shortly and all your canine buddies will be taken away to, if all goes according to my instructions, eventually find their freedom. We, on the other hand, are very much in danger from both sides, the cats and the dogs."

"For dogness' sake! What is that filthy rodent squawking about?!" commented Gilbert with an indignant huff.

"You're going to have to trust me, Gilbert. I'll explain later, assuming we ever get out of here." Billy, seeing the Min Pin relax his hostile posturing fumbled to unhook her friend's leash.

"That's enough of the talk, two-foot," urged Algernon. "We have to hurry it up. This ship is starting to fire its landing rockets."

Free of his chain Gilbert shook his matted coat and tried to ignore the insults cast by the other terriers, who called him traitor and demanded their money back.

Dashing through the ship with the mouse in the lead and Billy taking up the rear, the three hurried to recapture the Rocket of H.O.P.E. which Algernon knew to be stored just inside the flagship's tremendous main hatch.

"You know," commented Billy as they

rushed along, "it wouldn't surprise me if you two became good friends. Wouldn't that be nice?"

There was a immediate cackle from both Gilbert and Algernon.

Still laughing, the Min Pin commented, "She really is a typical two-foot."

"Just like all the rest," answered Algernon, shaking its head in resignation.

Billy was first to spy her ship. She joyfully whispered, "Look, up ahead. Oh, it really is a rocket of hope."

"How are we going to get past those guards?" groaned Gilbert, who was next to see the spacecraft.

Algernon smugly enlightened his companions. "You'll be pleased to know that I've made careful study of the feline mind and that will be the key to our escape. Let me explain. If a typical cat falls off a table and hits his head on a bowl of food, for the rest of his life that cat will have the belief, somewhere in the back of his underutilized brain, that falling off a table and hitting your head makes food appear. In the science of the mind we call that a trigger memory. That said, I have a theory that confusion also acts as a common trigger amongst all cats. So here's what we do..."

After a short huddle, during which Algernon, Billy and Gilbert threw thoughtful glances towards the prowling guards, their plan was set. The Min Pin had one final protest but was quickly overruled by the others.

"Alright, we start on the count of three," directed Billy, who was already on her hands and knees watching the mouse fidgeting by the dog's side. "Come on, Algernon. Get mounted up!" the girl urged.

"He's not letting me," complained the mouse with an insulting look at the Min Pin.

"It's just so undignified—" began the terrier, ready to renew his objection.

Billy swallowed her impatience. "Okay, Gilbert. It's your choice, but think carefully. You can wait here to face the hundreds of terriers who would rip you apart to get their money back, assuming the cats don't claw us all to shreds first, or you can do your part to help us escape."

Gilbert forced a smile and lowered himself to the cold metal deck. "Time to mount up, little mousy!"

Jumping onto the Min Pin's back Algernon complimented Billy's use of psychology. "I have heard of using the carrot and the stick as form of motivation but you just used two sticks and virtually no carrot at all. Very clever!"

"Thanks, I'm not bad for a two-foot, eh?" Billy giggled. Then trotting on all fours the girl dashed towards the cats guarding her rocket.

Algernon quietly whispered to his impatient mount. "Wait for it. Wait for it. Wait..." The mouse and the jittery dog beneath him watched Billy dash like a crazed cow around the stunned guards. "Moo! Moo! Moo!—"

"Steady, Gilbert. Eighth moo, that's our cue... six, seven and... now!"

The mouse spanked the Min Pin's rear with a boisterous "Giddy-yap!" The dog bolted and began to chase Billy in sweeping circles. Algernon, holding tight to the dog's neck, waved a lasso made with a wire he had pulled from a door motor. "Yahoo!" the rodent shouted repeatedly, twirling the rope.

The stupefied guards watched the

bizarre rodeo consisting of dog, mouse and human. In very short order the cats assumed they were having a weird dream. Algernon was right! The felines, responding to their common trigger, lay down one by one and closed their eyes.

The three performers kept up their act until they were sure the guards were deep in slumber. Satisfied they would not wake, Billy and her theatrical troupe tiptoed aboard the recaptured spacecraft, securing the hatch tightly behind them.

Safe inside the rocket there was no time for the three to enjoy their success. Gilbert jumped to his control panel ready to hit the launch buttons while Billy took up the tiller to steer. Algernon, taking charge, instructed, "We will have just a few seconds between the time the flagship touches down and the big hatch opens.

When it does we have to zip out as fast as we can before the guards on the ground realize something is wrong and shoot us down. Alright? Any time now..."

"Wait!" cried Billy, remembering as she stepped in something stinky. "Where are the puppies?"

"The what?" Gilbert and Algernon inquired together.

"The three puppies! They weren't in the jail and they're not here!"

"No time to look, sorry, too bad," the dog frantically replied.

The mouse hurriedly offered, "The cats probably brought them up to the ship's kitchen. They like fresh tender puppy. Who knows if the little guys are even still—"

"I'm not leaving without them," Billy insisted.

"Are you nuts?" Gilbert's distress was evident.

But Algernon hastily agreed with the girl. "Okay, okay. Let's just take off as planned. If the pups haven't been eaten I know how we can get them back."

The mouse's assurance was good enough for Billy, who knew that so far the rodent had been true to his word.

Suddenly the cat's flagship touched down and a grey twilight edged in around the corners of its slowly opening hatch. "Any time now. Everybody ready?" the mouse nervously inquired.

The three held their breath until at last the rodent shouted, "Now!"

With that Gilbert hit the launch buttons. As the jet boosters belched their gritty clouds Billy guided the quivering ship through the narrow, half-open hatch.

The assault of smoke and noise from the rocket as it swished past caught the gun-toting cats on the ground completely by surprise, causing them to scatter across the landing pad. It was just as Algernon had hoped.

Now came cheers of joy and relief from the Billy and her companions even though they knew there was more danger ahead.

"Still want to rescue those puppies?" Algernon cried.

"Yes!" Billy shouted desperately above the noise.

"Yes!" barked the Min Pin, suddenly thirsting more danger.

"Alright then. Billy, start circling the flagship as tightly as you dare. I need you to lay down the thickest cloud of smoke you can to hide our next maneuver. Rat dog, I mean Gilbert, on my say so, I want you to cut power to all but the small steering thrusters. We are going to land about halfway up the flagship just outside the kitchen. If the pups are anywhere, I'm guessing, that's where they'll be!"

"But how will we get inside to rescue them?" Billy asked worriedly.

Gilbert smiled. "This ship was designed by felines for felines. Could you imagine they would build a kitchen that didn't have a cat door? Now, go where I tell you to and leave the rest to me!"

With the thick smoke still hiding it from the scattered guards below, the Rocket of H.O.P.E. was brought to a standstill as Algernon instructed. As quickly as his four small paws could scurry the mouse was outside and dashing through the flapping door cut in the flagship's side.

At first the worried rodent thought he

was too late, for the pups were nowhere to be seen. But then Algernon heard a whimpering from underneath the cover of a large gold plated chafing dish. Moving quickly he pried the lid open with a long wooden spoon. At first the pups were too dazed by the sudden light to move, but when they focused enough to see the mouse, who, it might be mentioned, was deliberately taunting them to action, their terrier instincts took over. Running for his life, Algernon was barely able to keep ahead of the three baby canines as they chased him across the kitchen, out the cat door and up into the waiting rocket. The exhausted rodent wasted no time in leaping to the safety of Billy's shirt collar, shouting breathlessly to Gilbert, "Shut the squeakin' hatch. Blast off!"

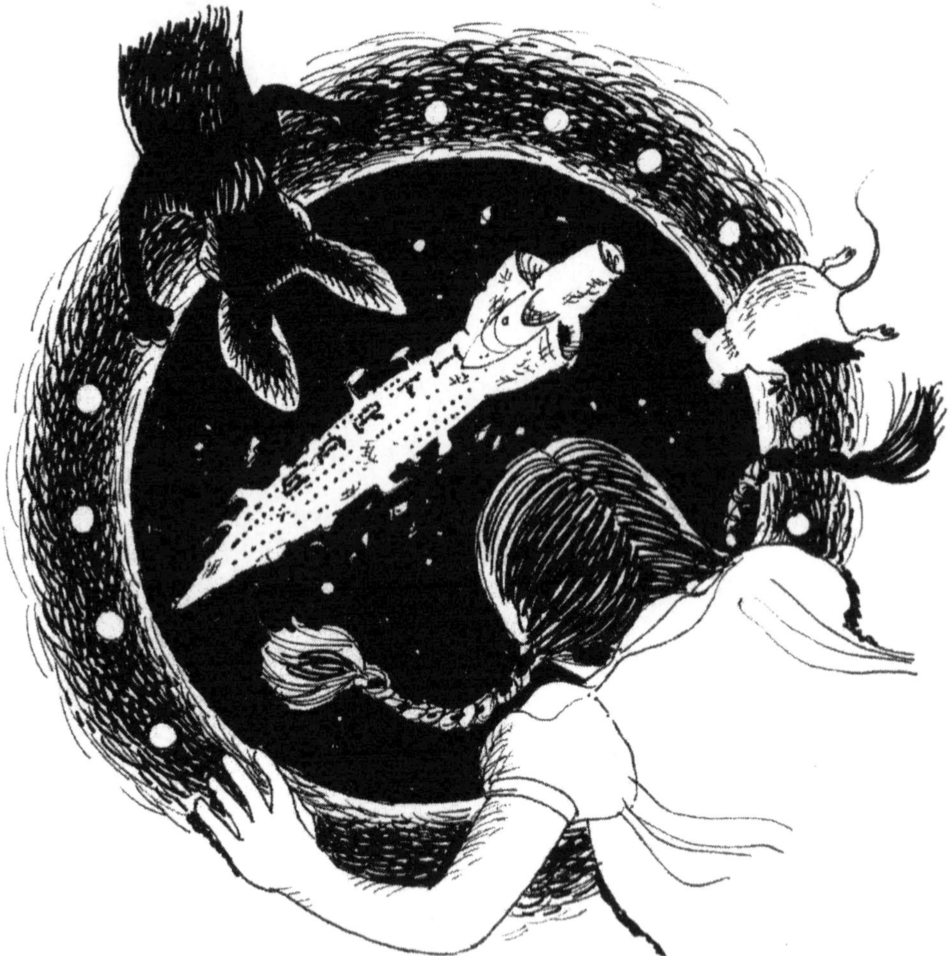

Chapter 11

"Well," thought Gilbert.

"Well," thought Algernon, echoing the dog.

"Well," thought Billy, continuing the thoughts of the others, "as long as we understand what we are in for, we could try to get there."

It had been a week since the daring escape from the *H.M.S. Cheshire* and Woof World. Gilbert, upon discovering that the war was a complete sham and that he was no richer as a result of all his efforts, was beyond himself with grief. Having been in the live-dog fur trade the Min Pin knew he could never return home, leaving him at a complete loss as to what his future might hold. Algernon, on the other hand, was just plain happy to enjoy the freedom of space and to be away from the constant worry that the possible discovery of his secret identity caused.

It was Billy who suggested to her new friends that they come with her to Earth where, as her parents had promised, a new life awaited. But Earth was still four-hundred and ninety-four years away. And there was no getting there so much as a minute faster, for as it turned out there was no such thing as Frisbee power. That energy source, Algernon disclosed, was something he had dreamed up during his little war game. Among other things it was a way of explaining to the rocket pilots and refugees why their space flights were so short.

"I feel like such a fool," Gilbert moaned.

"Not a fool to most, but to my superior mind I can see why—" began the mouse.

"Superior mind? Ha!" mocked the dog. "Why, I have more brainpower in the stump of my tail than you have in your whole rotten species!"

"For Pete's sake, will you two just cut it out?" shushed Billy, trying to shield the ears of the three snoozing pups in her lap. "These guys are just starting get language skills. The last thing I want is for them to end up as quarrelsome as you two."

Gilbert's and Algernon's faces turned apologetic. They probably would have continued to skulk but Billy announced that she felt something unfamiliar coming near. "Something's out there," she muttered mysteriously.

But the girl was not the only one to feel it, for as she peered into space Billy was joined at the porthole by Gilbert and Algernon.

"I don't see anything except stars," the mouse proclaimed, searching the blackness outside.

"Me neither, but still, I can feel it. Something *is* out there," added the Min Pin.

"That speck over there!" Billy indicated as she grabbed the tiller and steered the spaceship towards the dot that was starting to take shape. "It looks like another craft of some kind."

"Yes, there!" the mouse and dog chimed together.

The three waited with bated breath as the strange metallic tube drew closer. The pups, sensing something as well, awoke and stood in anticipation of what, no one knew.

Finally the mysterious thing slowly tumbled clearly before them. Reflecting the light of the nearest sun was a dulled silver rocket, a rounded point at one end and vestigial fins on the other. A dozen twisted and broken antenna protruded from the space-weary hull as the ship drifted aimlessly through space. Despite the many rows of windows on the unknown vessel all on the Rocket of H.O.P.E. gloomily sensed there was no longer life on board.

"Wait!" Billy exclaimed to the puzzled group. "There's some writing on the side. Big block letters. See?"

Algernon and Gilbert had to admit their eyes were not as good as the girl's and insisted, "What does it say? Please, tell us!"

"E-A-R-T-H," Billy read slowly. "It says Earth."

"What do you mean, Earth?!" demanded Gilbert. "That planet is four-hundred and ninety-six years away. Why would Earth have a ship out here?"

Algernon, with his superior brain, did

not have to read the girl's thoughts to know the answer. The rodent suggested, "Billy, perhaps you should be the one to explain this..."

The mouse hopped up onto Billy's shoulder as the girl reached to sooth Gilbert with a scratch to his ear. "It means, my terrier friend, that a very long time ago the creatures of Earth were looking for a way to escape. For reasons we will never know, they were trying to leave their world."

The Min Pin stood motionless, absorbing the meaning of Billy's words. He then asked the *big* question. "If the Earthlings were trying to leave their planet way back then, what could we possibly find there for ourselves?"

Billy smiled soulfully. "I don't think we have to travel across the universe to find out, do we? There *is* nothing for us there."

Algernon twitched. "I think you're saying we're going home, right?"

"Maybe, Algernon," the girl thought for all to hear, "the lesson for us is to go improve the world we were trying to run away from." Billy wasn't sure.

"Hey, what about me? I surely can't go back where I came from," protested the dog.

Billy and the mouse looked at each other and then at Gilbert.

"I suppose," mused the girl good-naturedly, "if you behave yourself you can come with us."

Algernon added with a grin, "Besides, we can't just drop these helpless pups off on Woof World with no one to guide them. They'll need a safe place and a guardian to raise them right. Perhaps when they are grown up—"

"So, I can come with you? I'll be a

really good baby-sitter and I won't ask for a dime!" chortled the relieved Min Pin, turning to the wagging fuzz balls. "I swear, little pups, I'll take really good care of—" Gilbert didn't finish. He was under attack by the three appreciative tongues slobbering his face.

It only took a few minutes after the Earth ship drifted past for Billy and Algernon to reset their rocket's course towards home. Gilbert took up his chew toy as the six traveling companions curled cozily together. Billy then reached up to the control that would put them all to sleep for the journey.

"Ready? Here we go!" the girl announced, twisting the purple dial.

"What do you think we should do when we get home?" asked the mouse as he waited for sleep to come.

"Well," said Billy, as though she had already given it a lot of thought. "There is this place I know. It's called an amusement park. Something tells me if we could get it running—" But then she and the others were fast asleep.

Billy, Gilbert, Algernon and the three puppies would have another six years to dream about the world they would make. And who knows what ideas they would come up with by then?

130

Epilogue

Upon their safe arrival, Billy and her companions set to the task of rebuilding the amusement park using the freshly painted Rocket of H.O.P.E. as its centerpiece.

Algernon, with his media savvy, began a vigorous advertising campaign calling the renewed playland *W.O.O.F.L.A.N.D.* which stood for *World Of Onederful Fun Let's All Njoy Dis*. Alright, just because the mouse was brilliant doesn't mean he was a good speller.

The restored park proved wildly popular as a place where parents could bring their super-powerless children. A small world in which to enjoy themselves and feel perfectly normal.

Of course Gilbert, using his extensive experience with refugees, taught his foster puppies the art of money and crowd control.

With the four of them working together *W.O.O.F.L.A.N.D.* was run like a pretty well-oiled machine.

Because the amusement park was such an immediate and popular success it would have looked bad for the World Government to do anything other than give it their full blessing. Now calling the *defective* kids *special,* the leaders permitted a city for the children and their families to be built in the surrounding swamps.

Within a few short years other amusement parks opened all over the world coupled with new cities as well.

It took another generation of children but it was finally admitted by everyone that the world's population was slowly returning to normal. The super power experiment was, in the long run, a failure. The world was again on the brink of crisis.

Then one day an idea came to Billy, now a mother herself. With the help of Algernon's great-great-grandmice she appeared on televisions around the globe.

"Tomorrow morning," Billy Peasoup-Casserole said, smiling into the camera with her own children close around her, "tomorrow morning, everyone should just walk to the nearest job."

Though the suggestion was hardly practical, it was a beginning.

*****

Author Neal Evan Parker was born in Brooklyn, New York in 1956. While sailing the waters of New England as a teenager, Neal became devoted to traditional sailing vessels. By the age of 20 he was a licensed captain. Since then Parker has skippered over a dozen schooners and traditional craft. In 1986 Captain Parker purchased and restored the 67-foot schooner *Wendameen*. Dedicating four years to her restoration, he placed the schooner into the Maine windjammer business. In April 2005, after a run of almost 20 years, Capt. Neal Parker sold his beloved vessel. With many books published and more on the way Parker is now devoting his time to professional ship model work, writing and being a full time father.

Also by Neal Evan Parker and available on Amazon.com

The Strange Perils of Ruth and Hawkins – *Book One ~ The Blue Lobster* - This is the first volume in a series of thrillers for young readers. Taking place on the coast of Maine the two heroes encounter adventures both natural and supernatural.

The Lobsterman And The U.F.O. – The story of a craggy old lobsterman and his encounter with a visitor from "away".

Captain Annabel – A fully illustrated children's story about a young girl who grows up to become master of her own tugboat.

The Adventures of Captain Annabel - Contained in this volume is a fuller account of Annabel's rise to command of her own tugboat and her subsequent adventures... and stay tuned for the next volume *Captain Annabel - Flying Colours.*

***Wendameen*, Life of an American Schooner** - An historical and autobiographical account of Captain Neal Parker and his famous schooner.

Around Cape Horn – Edited from the 1892 journals of maritime artist and historian Charles Davis.

The Fisherman of Kinsale - the misadventure of an Irish fisherman who refuses to be outdone... A classic story retold.

Artist Jim Sollers is a native of Maryland who has called Maine his home for more than twenty years. Originally trained in fine art, Jim is sought after as both a fine artist and illustrator specializing in marine themes. More recently Mr. Sollers has garnered acclaim for his artwork in nature books and children's stories. In the world of fine art his paintings are highly prized in private collections in the U.S. and abroad. For this edition of *The Butcher's Pig* Mr. Sollers has kept the illustrations spontaneous with simple pencil drawings. He has a true knack for capturing both moments and body language. Jim Sollers also illustrated other books by Parker including, *The Adventures of Captain Annabel*, *The Lobsterman and the U.F.O.*, *The Butcher's Pig* and *The Strange Perils of Ruth and Hawkins*.

Made in the USA
Middletown, DE
16 July 2017